W9-CBR-395

Ann Beneduce, Consulting Editor

Printed in Hong Kong by South China Printing Co.
(1988) Ltd.

The text is set in 20-point GillSans.
The art was done in painted tissue-paper collage.

Library of Congress Cataloging-in-Publication Data
Carle, Eric.
"Slowly, slowly, slowly," said the sloth / Eric Carle.
p. cm.
Summary: Challenged by the other jungle animals for its seemingly lazy
ways, a sloth living in a tree explains the many advantages of his slow and
peaceful existence.
[1. Sloths—Fiction. 2. Jungle animals—Fiction. 3. Animals—Fiction.] I. Title.
PZ7.C21476 SI 2002
[E]—dc21   2002016057
ISBN 0-399-23954-5
10 9 8 7 6 5 4 3 2 1
First Impression

For Ute and Gerhard

Jane Goodall visiting Eric Carle in his studio.

© Mary Lewis

About the Sloth
by Jane Goodall

Sloths have fascinated me ever since, when I was a child, I learned about their existence in the jungles of South America. There are two species—the three-toed and the two-toed. Sloths can turn their heads about 270 degrees. They can also hang from one leg and rotate their bodies, in a manner most horrifying to observe, through almost 360 degrees. They spend their lives upside down, hanging from the branches. They feed, mostly at dawn and dusk, on shoots and blossoms, leaves and fruits. After feeding for a few hours, moving slowly from one branch to the next, they fall asleep. They sleep fifteen to nineteen hours out of twenty-four, hanging from a branch with their heads laid on their bellies. They look just like a part of the tree because a kind of green algae grows in strange grooves on their long, coarse hairs, so that they become the same greenish color as their forest world; all kinds of moths and beetles live in their fur. If the sloths are threatened, they defend themselves by striking out with their powerful arms and daggerlike claws.

Sloths live in the same tree for days, sometimes weeks. About once a week, looking fat, they climb slowly down to the ground, where they defecate and urinate, carefully bury their waste, and climb slowly back—looking slim! When they do move to a new tree, they may have to swim across a river—they are surprisingly fast swimmers. Sloths are silent animals. Occasionally they comment on life with a gentle sigh that sounds like "ah-ee."

When I was a child, sloths, although they were sometimes hunted for food by the indigenous people, had little else to fear. Today they face the destruction of their habitat as forests are cut down for timber or to create grazing land for cattle. I am so delighted that my friend Eric Carle has chosen to write this book about a sloth. It will do so much to make young people aware of these delightful, gentle, peace-loving creatures. And as more and more people care, so there is greater hope that the sloths, along with their forest world and the other wondrous creatures that live there, will survive.

Eric Carle

"Slowly, Slowly, Slowly," said the Sloth

Philomel Books   New York

Slowly,
      slowly,
            slowly,
a sloth crawled
along a branch of a tree.

Slowly,
   slowly,
      slowly,
the sloth ate a leaf.

Slowly,
    slowly,
        slowly,
the sloth fell asleep.

Slowly,
slowly,
slowly,
the sloth woke up.

All day long
the sloth hung
upside down
in the tree.

All night long
the sloth hung
upside down
in the tree.

Even when it rained
the sloth hung
upside down
in the tree.

"Why are you so slow?"
the howler monkey asked one day.

But the sloth didn't answer.

"Why are you so quiet?"
the caiman asked.

But the sloth didn't answer.

"Why are you so boring?"
the anteater asked.

But the sloth didn't answer.

"Tell me," said the jaguar,
"why are you so lazy?"

The sloth thought
and thought
and thought
for a long, long, long time.

Finally, the sloth replied,
"It is true that I am slow, quiet
and boring. I am lackadaisical,
I dawdle and I dillydally.
I am also unflappable, languid,
stoic, impassive, sluggish,
lethargic, placid, calm, mellow,
laid-back and, well, slothful!
I am relaxed and tranquil,
and I like to live in peace.
But I am not lazy."
Then the sloth yawned and said,
"That's just how I am.
I like to do things
        slowly,
            slowly,
                slowly."

Toucan

Armadillo

Postman
Butterfly

Hoatzin

Anaconda

Poison
Dart
Frog

Anteater

Bat

Yellow-Spotted
River Turtle

Peccary

Puma

Tapir